FAST CARS

aston
MARTIN

by Randal C. Hill

Reading Consultant:
Barbara J. Fox
Reading Specialist
North Carolina State University

Content Consultant:
James Elliott
Editor
Classic & Sports Car magazine

Capstone
press

Mankato, Minnesota

Blazers is published by Capstone Press,
151 Good Counsel Drive, P.O. Box 669, Mankato, Minnesota 56002.
www.capstonepress.com

Library of Congress Cataloging-in-Publication Data
Hill, Randal C.
    Aston Martin / by Randal C. Hill.
    p. cm.—(Blazers. Fast cars)
    Includes bibliographical references and index.
    ISBN-13: 978-1-4296-0097-2 (hardcover)
    ISBN-10: 1-4296-0097-7 (hardcover)
    1. Aston Martin automobile—Juvenile literature. I. Title. II. Series.
TL215.A75H55 2008
629.222—dc22   2007004903

Summary: Simple text and colorful photographs describe the history and models
    of the Aston Martin.

Essential content terms are **bold** and are defined at the bottom of the page
where they first appear.

Editorial Credits
Mandy Robbins, editor; Bobbi J. Wyss, designer; Jo Miller, photo researcher

Photo Credits
Alamy/Mark Scheuern, 17
Corbis/Andrew Fox, 6; Car Culture, 11 (top), 13 (bottom), 16, 26–27, 28–29;
    James L. Amos, 7; Reuters/Denis Balibouse, 14–15; Sygma/Yassukovich, 24;
    Tim Graham, 22–23
Dreamstime, 4–5
Getty Images Inc./Hulton Archive, 8–9
The Image Works/NMPFT/Kodak Collection/SSPL, 12
NetCarShow.com, 11 (bottom)
Ron Kimball Stock/Ron Kimball, cover, 10 (top), 13 (top), 18–19
Shutterstock/Massimiliano Lamagna, 25
SuperStock Inc./Roger Allyn Lee, 10 (bottom)
ZUMA Press/Harvey Schwartz, 20–21

1 2 3 4 5 6 12 11 10 09 08 07

TABLE OF CONTENTS

chapter 1
QUALITY CARS

When an Aston Martin hits the road, heads turn. Aston Martins add power and class to smooth lines. They are among the world's finest sports cars.

Aston Martin DB9

Each car is built by hand in Gaydon, England. Buyers choose the car's body color, seat trim, and other details. It takes about eight weeks to build these dream machines.

fast fact

In Britain, a car's hood is called the bonnet. The boot is its trunk.

Lionel Martin

Hill climb race, 1922

TWO DETERMINED DREAMERS

Englishman Lionel Martin sold cars in the early 1900s. But his real interest was in hill climb racing. In this sport, cars race up steep hills.

ASTON MARTIN TIMELINE

Martin's friend Robert Bamford shared his love of cars. The two men decided to build the fastest, most stylish cars in England.

The DB4 is released.

1958

1922

Aston Martin passenger cars go on sale.

1932

Aston Martin Le Mans is introduced.

1947

David Brown buys Aston Martin company. DB models begin to be made in his honor.

In 1913, they formed Bamford and Martin Limited. Martin raced the first cars at Aston Hill. For that reason, the cars were called Aston Martins.

Aston Martin DB 9

Ford Motor Company buys Aston Martin.

1994

2004

1977

2007

Three current models go on sale.

Ford sells Aston Martin to a group of businessmen.

V8 Vantage is released.

Aston Martin race car, 1923

The first Aston Martins were race cars. Passenger cars weren't sold until 1922. Aston Martins have been amazing drivers around the world ever since.

1959 Aston Martin DB4

1979 Aston Martin V8

chapter 3

PEAK
PERFORMANCE

Aston Martin's V8 Vantage is a perfect mix of power and style. This bold sports car can reach 62 miles (100 km) per hour in only 5 seconds.

2005 Aston Martin DB9

The DB9's body is ***aerodynamic***.
Its wide wheelbase creates more passenger
room and a smooth ride. The DB9 can
speed to 186 miles (300 km) per hour.

aerodynamic — **built to
move easily through the air**

The most powerful Aston Martin is the 520-**_horsepower_** Vanquish S. Its engine roars from zero to 62 miles (100 km) per hour in 4.8 seconds.

horsepower — a unit that measures an engine's power

Aston Martin DB9 interior

ASTON MARTIN VANQUISH S DIAGRAM

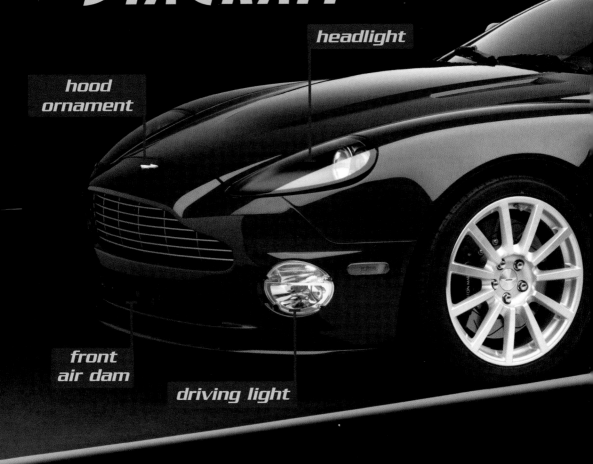

headlight

hood ornament

front air dam

driving light

door mirror

wheel

19

chapter 4

UNIQUE MODELS

Lots of thought goes into making each model different. Fifty designs were tested before the V8 Vantage hit the market.

The DB9 Volante is Aston Martin's only **convertible**. Its power top can be put up or down in 17 seconds.

convertible — a car with a top that can be put up or down

Britain's Prince Charles owns several Aston Martins.

The Vanquish S looks like
an animal about to attack. Hand
paddles by the steering wheel
shift its six-speed *transmission*.

transmission — a series of gears that send power from the engine to the wheels; the higher the gear is, the faster the car can go.

chapter 5

WORKS OF ART

Aston Martins are first-class sports cars. They are made of strong, lightweight materials and have the newest technology.

2006 Rapide Concept from Aston Martin

1959 DB4 (green), 1958 DB Mark III (blue), and 1979 V8 (red)

Aston Martins are built to last. About 75 percent of the cars sold since 1922 are still on the road!

fast fact

James Bond drove an Aston Martin in all of the Bond movies.

GLOSSARY

aerodynamic (air-oh-dye-NAM-mik)—built to move easily through the air

convertible (kuhn-VUR-tuh-buhl)—a car with a top that can be lowered or removed

horsepower (HORSS-pou-ur)—a unit for measuring an engine's power

transmission (transs-MISH-uhn)—a series of gears that send power from the engine to the wheels

READ MORE

Doeden, Matt. *Sports Cars.* Horsepower. Mankato, Minn.: Capstone Press, 2005.

Donovan, Sandy. *Sports Cars.* Motor Mania. Minneapolis: Lerner, 2007.

Oxlade, Chris. *Sports Cars.* Mean Machines. Chicago: Raintree, 2005.

INTERNET SITES

FactHound offers a safe, fun way to find Internet sites related to this book. All of the sites on FactHound have been researched by our staff.

Here's how:
1. Visit *www.facthound.com*
2. Choose your grade level.
3. Type in this special code **1429600977** for age-appropriate sites. You may also browse subjects by clicking on letters, or by clicking on pictures or words.
4. Click on the **Fetch It** button.

FactHound will fetch the best sites for you!

INDEX